1

Contents

Poetic Reflections

Make beautiful expressions of the heart

They tell it like it is…in a rhyme scheme that slips it by easy

Author: Wesley J Allen

Publisher: Artistic Word Creations
All rights reserved

First copy of 1st edition sold 5-15-97
First copy of 2nd edition sold 2-24-04
First copy of 3rd edition sold 8-20-11

Alphabetical Index

SECTION ONE – LOVE AND BEAUTY

Til Death DoUs Part

This represents my heart, big and grand;
and it's yours forever because you are my friend.
We've been together now for fifteen years.
We've had lots of laughs, and shed many tears.

When I consider all you've been to me during this time,
I think of the excellent wife Solomon describes.
You are worth more to me than fine jewels; and
for you I'd give up all of my wood king tools.

Happy is the man with a quiver full of children.
You've certainly given me that; they're worth more than a million.
I try to teach the kids Bible, from the knowledge in my head,
that isn't very smart; because you're the one who shows them
Jesus by the love in your heart.

You always try to keep my hopes up when things are going bad
You've struggled to take the place of my mom and my dad.
Yes my darling, I give you my whole heart.
And I hope we're together til death do us part

                                                            6-15-89

This is the 1st poem I ever wrote that I thought
was worth keeping. I framed it on a red background in a beautiful lacewood, heart-shaped
picture frame and presented it to my wife on
our 15th anniversary. I couldn't read it, and she
couldn't listen without tears in our eyes. I wrote
it six months after our separation, with hope,
while I sat on the fence and waited to see which
way our relationship would go. All the while I
was working on me. On the next page is a song
that will give you a hint as to which way it went.

7

The Fires of My Heart

Dorcy, Darling, you lit the fires of my heart.
You melted it together where it was broke apart.
I never thought in all my life I'd feel like this again.
You helped me climb up from the pits and now my heart can
mend.

Dorcy, Darling, you are a friend of mine.
My heart longs to be with you just about all the time.
Come and share your life with me and we'll float on the air.
It'll be like Heaven on the Earth just as long as you are there.

Dorcy, Darling, you make me feel like I want to dance.
My lips are singing all day long; in my heart we're making
romance.
I hope I make you feel just as good as you do me.
I want to light the fires of your heart and let you float upon
the breeze.

Dorcy, Darling, you lit the fires of my heart.
You melted it together where it was broke apart.
I never thought in all my life I'd feel like this again.
Yes, you kindled the fires of my heart!
You kindled the fires of my heart!
Yes, you kindled the fires of my heart!

9-13-90

The Beautiful Goddess

She's a beautiful lady, like the goddess called Venus.
She's got the power over my heart.
And I hope that love's chain will bind us together
that nothing can tear us apart.

Her smile's like the sunshine. Her green eyes intrigue me.
They captivate my heart and my mind.

8

She's so sweet that her lips drip with honey,
and I think about her all the time.

Her voice is like music, sweet singing of Angels,
and I love the thrill that I get
when we sit and talk hour after hour.
She's the nicest girl I've ever met!

She has a beautiful, kind, Christian spirit,
more lovely than I've ever known;
and I certainly have been enjoying
all the love toward me that she's shown.

7-5-91

Moments of Bliss

I have a message to give to my princess
to let her know where my thoughts abide.
The perfect place and the perfect time
God himself will provide.

Taking a stroll through a garden of flowers
with my princess at my side.
Admiring the beauty of God's creation.
Speaking of the blessings that are mine.

With blue eyes sparkling like crystal waters,
long, golden hair rippling in the breeze,
she told me I did a wonderful job
on my early-morning speech.

She's like a godly girl from Little House on the Prairie.
Her long skirt dances in the breeze.
The blossoms of flowers I placed in her hands
are scarcely more beautiful than she.

Capturing the glory of the moment.

Taking both of her hands in mine.
I said, "It will be the ultimate blessing
if He'll bless me with you for my bride."

Then we walk toward her elegant chariot,
finished with the morning's first deeds.
Straight and true on the wings of an angel
the black stallion will give it speed.

Sitting within her chariot,
savoring the moments of bliss,
softly I tell her I love her
and we share a holy kiss.

10-29-98

I Never Fell in Love with You

I never fell in love with you;
but it grew right from the start.
I never fell in love with you;
but you've totally won my heart.

I didn't want to get to know you.
The first impression was negative.
But since I'm kind to everyone;
I gave you what I had to give.

You were burdened with a load of stress.
The road to freedom is paved with grace.
I gave the message God gave to me,
that released me from all the pain.

I never fell in love with you;
but it grew right from the start.
I never fell in love with you;
but you've totally won my heart.

We got together so many times.
We fasted and we prayed.
We got to know each other well
when we talked the hours away.

Now, you're always in my heart
and always on my mind.
I know a more godly woman
would be terribly hard to find.

I never fell in love with you;
but it grew right from the start.
I never fell in love with you;
but you've totally won my heart.

11-11-98

11

Whispers of Wonder

Oh what a wonder that so long ago
God created the beauties of Earth.
A delightful pleasure it is for sure
that to humans and beasts He gave birth.

It's simply splendid to gaze into the heavens
and marvel at the wonders of night.
Or sit in the sun in the heat of the day
and feel the power of that life-giving light.

What pleasure to roam through gardens of flowers
beneath shady cottonwood trees,
and experience the glory of dozens of colors,
and see the birds that float on the breeze.

There are wonders in clouds, in blue skies, in rainbows,
in rocks, in caves, and in natural springs.
There's beauty along highways, through rivers, in valleys,
and in the intricate pattern of Dragonfly wings.

There are many more beauties, and many more wonders,
but none so lovely and precious
as those that are seen in the eyes of God's people
as they shine with the love of our Jesus.

And as for you, precious child of God,
it is seen in the smile of your face,
that your heart's filled with love, and kindness, and goodness,
and you're blessed with the richness of His grace.

There are wonders about you, and beauties, and more,
and it's a hope that for many more years,
we'll be blessed with the privilege of sharing your life,
your hopes, your joys, and your tears.

8-6-91

A Beautiful Wish

I hope and I wish,
and sometimes wishes come true,
for everything that's precious in life
to rain in torrents on you.

Sweet, pleasant fragrance of Spring,
genesis of life anew,
born in the hearts of all God's people
sparkles like the honey dew.

The deer drinks from a babbling brook,
bluebonnets wave from a thousand hills,
may all the beauty God gave creation
sing from your heart in thrills.

Your quiver is full, your children are near,
the memories of life most dear;
may all be peace and joy in your heart
and bring visions of Heaven here.

5-20-93

Cupid's Arrow

You shot an arrow from Cupid's bow
and it pierced my fragile heart,
making love flow rich and pure
to leave its crimson mark.

So every life I touch today
can be blessed by the Savior's grace,
as through me flows, by the Spirit of God,
radiant beams from the Master's face

He is the Lily of the Valley,
The Rose of Sharon true,
and by the power of the love of God,

13

has blessed my life through you.

Many times in the last few years
I wanted to fly into your arms,
experience the warmth of a mother's love,
feeling safe from the world's harms.

Yes, I will be your Valentine,
returning Cupid's arrow too,
because you are my precious Mom,
and that's why I love you.

2-14-92

> Written to my mother in
> Response to a Valentine
> I received from her.
> The poem above is a
> Mother's Day wish

Hi Darling:

Merry Christmas! Good Morning!
I love You, my Dear.
Wait til you see what
You're getting this year!
Take a stroll with me, Darling,
Out in the breeze.
When You see what awaits You
I know You'll be pleased.

ANTICIPATION is making me wait…

> Written at the request
> of Sidney Shaw to let
> her husband, Bill,
> know
> where to find his
> Christmas present.

Surprise, Dear!
I Love You! 12-23-93

14

Elizabeth

Elizabeth's a town
in the Natural State
at the tip of Norfork Lake,
twenty miles from the border
of the Show Me State
in the Bible Belt U.S.A.

Elizabeth's a gal
in the singles group
at the Richland Hills Church of Christ.
She abides with those
bound for the Glory Land
doing alms in The Master's sight.

It's a blessing
to visit Elizabeth
where some of God's people reside.
It's a joy to know Elizabeth
In whom God's Spirit abides.

4-12-92

My Beautiful Friend

You're as lovely and pretty as a flower
created by the hand of God.
You're as dainty and graceful as a butterfly
when it alights on a Goldenrod.

You're as sweet and nice as ever they come.
Few treat me as good as you do.
When sunrays grow dim and clouds cover the light
you help turn my gray skies to blue.

You've helped me through many a troublesome time
with encouraging words and a smile.
To your rescue I'd come, if your world fell in,
over stones, with bare feet, for a mile.

I certainly hope that we'll always be friends
until from this Earth we depart,
and even thereafter in our home in the sky,
you'll always be dear to my heart.

3-13-92

15

The Presence of Angels

A Marriage is made in the presence of Angels
when two loving hearts are united as one,
long before purchasing the gold wedding band
or making the promise, for better or worse.

On the day that you met, her eyes told the story.
They had searched the world over for one just like you.
God blessed the joy of the bonding that followed
as, in time, you developed a love sweet and true.

Now, no one else can compare to this Wildwood Flower,
her beauty and charm ranking far above all.
There was never a girl more perfectly fitting,
as you too, did your searching through the great and the
small.
God's Angels are gathering in The Garden of Prayer.
The soft, sweet notes of the wedding bells chime.
Anticipation grips this eager young couple,
believing, yet wondering, "Am I doing the right-thing this
time?"

Written to bless
Laura Davenport
and Larry McCune
for their wedding.

2-21-2002

16

The Most Wonderful Moment

When out of the bridal chamber she stepped
like a flower that springs into bloom,
the sun accenting the gold in her hair,
her glance met the eyes of her groom.

The day had finally come. The hour was here.
The minutes were ticking away.
Only to make it through the eyes of the crowd...
Her lips moved as she silently prayed.

Her groom stood majestic, patient, and poised.
Never had she seen him so elegantly sharp.
But so far away, across the ocean of faces,
fear was touching the eyes of her heart.

Her maids had worked hard to make perfect the moment.
She was more beautiful than he'd ever seen.
The eyes of his heart were moved with emotion.
running down his cheeks the evidence streamed.

This moment had been a long time in coming.
They'd been together for so many years.
"Lord, thank you for giving me this Wonderful Girl,"
his heart rejoiced through the streams of his tears.

The moment passed, as all moments will,
but it's one to be cherished forever.
Their promise of love, in the presence of God,
is a bond that no conflict can sever.

5-4-2002

Written to bless
Melissa & Michael
for their wedding.

17

Taking A Walk Along 543

Strolling along the narrow pavement,
digesting the beauty of the art of God,
soaking in sunshine on a summer morning,
we pick flowers, bounce stones, wait for Josh.

Color surrounds us in myriads of flowers.
The red and yellow ones Evelyn calls weeds.
But not even Solomon in all of his glory
was arrayed in splendor such as one of these.

A field of wheat nearly ripe unto harvest,
Larry just has to have a few plants.
Sends Wes traipsing through the deep, dense weeds
since he is the only one wearing pants.

Jared and Joshua skirt the perimeter
laughing and playing walkie talkie games.
Evelyn and Cyndi skip in a rhythm.
A ditch and a culvert have the interest of James.

Meanwhile, back at camp Bud studies the Word.
He already quotes more scripture than Wes
lying in the open out under the stars
while all the others try to get some rest.

Marly is resting and resisting the fudge.
Joe and Beverly leave for the Sunday School session.
Joanna's still putting her makeup on,
but she'll be there before the end of the lesson.

The girls investigate an old log cabin.
Josh and the guys stop to visit the Granny.
Wes gives her flowers and a nice little hug.
We look at pictures of all of her family.

We were all amazed with Grandma's garden,
Lettuce, Squash, and Corn are what she grows.
Pam loved the relaxing peace and tranquility,
and extended family living so close.

18

These gifts from the Lord we all enjoyed
along with the hospitality of the Covingtons too.
This poem was written with the earnest desire
to share our blessings and our joy with you.
6-13-92

Thank You, Lord, for: Joe & Beverly, Joanna, Grandma, Aunt Frances, Cousin Beck
From Us Campers:Josh, Bud, Jared, Joshua, Cyndi, Evelyn, Larry, James, Marly, Pam, Wes

The Keeper of Your Blessings

This neat little box will keep your Blessings
from loss, forgetfulness, or scatter.
In praising the Lord for His kindness and goodness,
you'll be doing what really matters.

With a box full of Blessings, you have stories to share,
casting smiles on streets of Uncertainty,
building a bridge over troubled waters,
eradicating the source of your worries.

Share your Blessings with all of your friends,
that they see the source of your strength.
And Bless the Lord with glory and honor,
and love Him with worship and praise.

The Carpenter's Workshop

12-18-2003

The Carpenter's Workshop is everyone's heart
when Jesus abides there-in.
He is The Carpenter, building His Kingdom,
perfecting you from within.

He sets you apart from the cares of the world,
makes your heart fit for His plan.
From a dull speck of dust, He makes you into a pearl
until you outshine every man.

We are all carpenters; we are His helpers,
in building The Kingdom grand,
sharing God's love with all those around us,
lending a helping hand.

Put away your hammer; stop polishing your nails,
your only tool is love.
There's no need to shape, grind, or chisel,
all perfecting comes from above.
Nothing bad ever happens to a carpenter
because we're always knocking on wood.
When you know The Carpenter, you can have most anything!
He makes all things work for good.

Angels Rejoice

Oh, the Angels rejoice in the Heavens above
when your prayers ascend to the throne of God's love.
Oh, the Angels rejoice, will rejoice even more,
when you do a kind deed in the name of the Lord.

When your prayers ascend to the throne of the Lord,
It empowers the Angels and sharpens their swords,
and they fight Satan's demons with the power of love,
and the Angels rejoice in the Heavens above.

When you do a kind deed and lift a friend's load
you help bear his burdens, bringing blessings untold.
When you give a kind word and bring peace to his heart
you destroy Satan's schemes and you tear them apart.

When you show love to a brother, though he unlovely may
seem,
the eyes of the Lord roam the Earth and He sees.
He will bless your life richly just to show that He cares,
and you escape being entangled in one of Satan's snares.
10-92

God's Highest Creation

May the pulse of my heart be your praise, oh Lord,
and the rhythm of my lungs sing your grace.
All my inner workings amaze me, on Lord,
I'm fearfully and wonderfully made.

From dust I was shaped in the depths of the Earth.
Skillfully each little organ was made.
Before the foundation of the world was laid
you planned the number of my days.
I love to be called your Highest Creation.
You know all of my thoughts and cares.
For me you care more than all of creation.
You know the number of all of my hairs.

My heart longs to walk with you, Lord,
like Enoch did when you took him home.
I want to explore the Heavens with you,
and the streets of pure gold to roam.

-1-94

Your Child I Am

May the cry of my heart reach your ears, oh Lord,
and the shine of your smile light my path.
I'm ready to heed your every instruction.
Your obedient child I am.

So long have I wandered, desire my guide,
and though it ended in crushing despair,
I was lifted up from the miry clay,
discovering you always are there.

22

Like a child serving his father, I stand.
I wonder at your wisdom and strength.
I believe, beyond doubt, that my life is ordered.
I walk in your footsteps by faith.

Oh, to trust you more than gravity.
You hold my feet on solid ground.
I know your love is forever dependable.
Though sinking, I cannot drown.

From this moment on, **You** are my life.
I'm buried with Him in the likeness of death.
I'm resurrected to walk in newness of life.
My spirit, apart from the world is set.

Like your own child you're raising me.
I have a desire for nothing more.
I know that I'm in the very best care.
All that I am is totally yours.

7-19-20

Written by request of the
Drama Ministry at Richland
Hills Church of Christ to be
included with other poetry in
one of their plays, and
signed: Anonymous

A child is helpless, dependent, loyal, compliant,
rebellious, foolish, needy, teachable, helpful, frail,
trusting, loyal, moldable, assured, defers judgment,
accepting, grateful, content, and has faith.
God wants us to be childlike in some ways,
but not childish in every way.

Eulogy

Through the beautiful Garden of Eden I walk,
where Adam and Eve once lived.
Angels in Heaven accompany me.

Oh, what for this life would you give?
There is no want here. There is no need.
God has established all of my ways.
He filled my heart overflowing with love.
He made me what I am today.

Once I walked through the Valley of the Shadow of Death,
tortured by night and by day.
Pain and anxiety were my faithful companions.
Tears were my constant wage.

At the end of the valley I found life's secret,
which unknown to me was there from the start.
Well cherished is the peace that surrounds me
at the quieting of my heart.

A surrender to love, to relinquish all fear
is the power that saved my life.
Anxiety washed away like sands from the seashore.
Like pigeons my troubles took flight.

This is my eulogy when I died to self
and though still on the earth I dwell,
satisfaction crowns my peaceful existence
since love's power has broken the spell.

2-12-2001

Surrender

I gave my heart to Jesus,
hung it on the cross.
That was many years ago,
but I didn't suffer loss.

He took my heart and made it grand,
multiplied its power.
Now He lives and works through me
every minute, every hour.

24

He added virtues to my life,
filled my heart with joy and peace.
My only purpose has become
love and forgiveness to give and receive.

My only goal is inner peace.
My mission, to share God's love.
All my prayers for all my friends
bring blessings from above.

When I go to live with Him,
within the jasper walls,
I want to see you there with me
so hearken to His call.

9-26-98

Spiritual Spinach

To the Lord I pray for spiritual spinach.
Conquering giants is a heavy task.
But the wonderful prize that's set before me
is beyond all that I could dream or ask.

Joyously I run to meet Goliath.
I'm more than conqueror through Jesus my Lord.
I can be struck down, but not destroyed.
Angels fight for me. Prayer sharpens their swords.
A giant is nothing but a G I ant
marching to the tune of the anthill queen.
Spiritual spinach is the word of God.
And faith is the evidence of things unseen.

He made a way through the lion's den.
He made a way through the raging sea.
And I know beyond a shadow of a doubt
that He will make a way for you and me.

10-7-98

The Thief's Cross is
Your Cross Too

25

Did you know, Dear One, that a man hung here
who was a precious child of God?
He was known to the world as a two-bit thief
for all the wrong he'd done.

But Jesus forgave him, cast his sins away,
and though as a consequence he died,
he accepted his wrong and bore his cross
now he lives in Paradise.

And you, Dear One, what was your crime?
Is there someone you've hurt?
The cross in the middle where Jesus died
raises your soul up out of the dirt.

He loves you, Dear One, with all of His heart,
and He certainly understands
all pressures in life, and the struggle and strife,
and the mischief in the heart of man.

If the cross is excessively heavy
that you seem forced to bear,
go east from the Garden to the good Lord's church
you'll find friends and comfort there.

I hope for the best for you, Dear One,
that God will bless you very much.
He sees your struggles; He knows your heart,
and He'll fill your life with love.

5-2-93

> Written in the Garden of Prayer, across the street
> from the Richland Hills Church of Christ, for the
> benefit of those
> who knocked down the Thief's Cross.

The Spiritual Aspects of Fishing
I arrived at the park for the Spring Retreat

anxiously anticipating who I'd meet,
drawn to the event by a serious quest
discover the spiritual aspects of fishing.

The guys were friendly; nature's beauty was great,
Serenity Point we called the fishing place.
I fished for an hour with never a bite;
so, where is the spiritual aspects of fishing?

We shared our food; we shared our lives,
we talked about losses by campfire light.
Then I slept out under the stars, dreaming
about the spiritual aspects of fishing.

On Serenity Point at the break of day
we heard a story about the Indian's ways.
Did a little bit of casting but I've still to
learn the spiritual aspects of fishing.

We did some artwork. Had a great time.
We talked about tools to change our lives.
But how in the world will I ever discover
the spiritual aspects of fishing?

We had a Pow Wow in the camp that night.
Shared poetry beside the campfire light.
Tomorrow we leave and I haven't seen
the spiritual aspects of fishing.

We talked about our feelings at the break of day.
We had some prayers before we went our way.
I want you to know that this whole story
tells the spiritual aspects of fishing.

Men sharing their lives amidst nature's glory,
caring for each other, and sharing their stories.
Even though we caught not even a minnow

this is the spiritual aspects of fishing.

4-22-94

Rest in Jesus

From The Garden of Prayer, in the beauty of Spring,
God beckons to me, while all nature sings,
come away with Me child from all worldly cares.
Share with Me your thoughts and your prayers.

Beauty, riches, everything is yours if you ask,
no matter what you've done in the past.
Observe My empty tomb!
Jesus, My son, was resurrected for you.

I'll be the bridge over this troubled life
only dine with Me by day **and** by night.
There is rest for your weary bones.
My shepherds will help; you're never alone.

I have walked above all the tempest and strife.
Now, the road to Golgotha leads to life.
The cross in the middle where Jesus died
is a symbol to dispel all of your pride.

You could never have made it alone
no matter what good things you have done.
So I give to you the way of escape
from sin, from struggle, from the laws I have made.

Rest in Jesus! He died because of your sins.
Surrender your struggle and let Him live.   4-26-2002

Heavenly Journey

I took a friend on a mental journey

28

into a state of deep relax.
We floated on clouds; we explored galaxies,
we visited The Glory Land.

We bowed low before the throne of God,
winged Angels on every hand.
We joined the singing in a choir of Saints,
and played in a Harp and Timbrel band.

We explored the Heavens on a street of gold,
viewing castles and mansions magnificent.
We praised God by every name I could think of.
He called us precious, and pure, and innocent.

We floated to Earth with Jesus between us,
held His hands and walked through a valley grand.
He showed us flowers, and new life, and beauty,
we felt the holes in both of His hands.

He told us to think of beauty and honor
and with us will be the God of Peace.
He filled us with power and love and acceptance,
and all the pain from our bodies released.

1-5-95

From My Heart to God's

Lord, my heart longs to walk with you
the way that Enoch did.
How I long to leave behind
all my desire for sin!
I want to talk with you by day,
rest in your arms at night.
Lord, grant that I can be with you
for all the rest of my life.

I chance to roam so far from you,
pressed against the outer wall.
Sin comes knocking at my door
and I can't hear you when you call.
My heart hurts with loneliness,
in the Valley of Despair.
The entire world sneers at me.
I can't find comfort anywhere.

Lord, my heart longs to walk with you
the way that Enoch did.
How I long to leave behind
all my desire for sin!
I want to talk with you by day,
rest in your arms at night.
Lord, grant that I can be with you
for all the rest of my life.

Mark Twelve – The Widow's Mite

In the Garden of Prayer I found two pennies.
They spoke of the Widow's Mite,
who into the treasury put two copper coins,
giving all she had in this life.

All around her were people with much,
who some from their surplus gave.
Jesus commended the Widow's worship,
giving her honor and praise.

Will you be as the Scribes in verse 38
or the Widow in forty three?
Will you keep all the best for yourself,
or give to those who have need?

Many have riches, popularity, and friends
while others are starved for some care.

Will you share all that you are and you have?
The Jesus-like spirit is rare!

Will you give your time, your knowledge, your love
to help those who struggle through life?
Of all the richness that you possess
it'll cost less than the Widow's Mite.

Meet with the Lord in The Garden of Prayer,
Let this be your trysting place.
Ask what it is He would have you to do.
Wait for His answer in faith.

8-4-92

31

SECTION THREE – FIRE AND BRIMSTONE

Dead to Self, Alive in Jesus

How many times were the prophets of God
ridiculed because they sang to a different tune?
How many times were they beaten or killed
by the wisdom of the scoffers rude?

Have you taken a seat amongst the scoffers?
Do you judge men by your standard of good?
A humble heart is the Lord's delight!
Have you honored Jesus whenever you could?

If I punished My people because of sin,
how many times would you have died?
What good that you hold above all else
would have protected you in your pride?

Do you think I'm impressed with commandment keepers?
What happened to Balaam before he died?
Did he not keep My every instruction?
But what evil, in his heart, did he hide?

If Jesus, My son, fulfilled the law
what precepts do you uphold?
Would it not be many times better
if your old-self lay under the waters dead and cold?

Your only command is to become a slave
of righteousness pure and sweet,
to live in Jesus, dead to self
is the commandment you must keep.

So put away your sword, the battle is Mine,
and it's not against flesh and blood.

Prepare the way for the Lord to make change.
Jesus did all that you could never have done. 5-10-2002

Cedar Boxes

Build me a cedar box, my friend.
Make it sixteen inches wide.
Cedar will stifle the stench of death
that reeks from the doctor's knife.

Yes, place them head to head, kind sir,
and stack them double high.
Bury them six feet deep, young man,
four bodies lying thigh to thigh.

Eight would be lives in a single box.
Yes, give them decent honor.
Wholesale death in a compact grave,
sentenced by Mama and the doctor.

At what point do you think Almighty God
breathed in the Spirit of life?
Only to be judged, then put to death,
snuffed out by the doctor's knife.

So, where will you go from here, young lass?
What will your verdict be?
Will your child be given a chance to live,
or and early eternity?3-16-92

In this poem the mortician speaks.
He isn't describing a very decent burial,
but it's better than the one these children
are likely to get. Kids, today, are killed
off by the dozens before they have a chance
to take their first breath. Won't you please
take a stand for kindness and goodness, Mama?
You are the judge! Your verdict counts!

I wrote this poem years ago
before my mind fully
developed spiritually. Now I
understand better why a
woman's choice should be
upheld. It is not good to
bring an unwanted child into
the world. And God would
agree with many of the
reasons for abortion.

For Sure   Written in response to Mary Oliver's "Maybe."
In tough-love, Jesus condemned
self-righteous, judgmental actions
of legal extortionists who controlled
the downtrodden for selfish gain.

Some followers will be saved that day,
freed from oppression that causes
churning emotions, boiling inwardly,
filling them with crippling physical pain.

Twill be something new and different
when the meek shall inherit the Earth, no more cowering
under the glance of self-righteous indignation
that makes one fear for his life and his loved ones.

Seventy years, perhaps eighty by strength,
we live, and just barely, under the controls
of some exalted above that which is good and righteous,
manipulating the "Law" to their advantage.

They never consider one even exists
who is greater, and demands an accounting
of all that was done and all that was taught
in the name of Meme, the King of a nation called Self.

Jesus, the Judge, is meek and loving and kind,
but shall only deal mercy where mercy was given
all others will writhe in the pain they inflicted
and death will be far from their grasp.

Many times more frightening than death
is the wrath of the one who holds power
to place the sheep on the right and goats on the left.
Are you sure of which place you'll stand?

Thank the Lord for large favors
there is always repentance, then justification,
the price has been paid, get your ticket
but don't wait at the entrance.

Get out there; spread tidings,
tell how you were freed, let your colleagues
have the same chance to turn their lives over
to the one who has the power to save.   3-31-92

Could Hell Be Like This?

What would be a more effective
 punishment for a sin,
than to put the sinner in front of the door
 and let him not walk in?

For the totally selfish alcoholic
who lived only for the bottle he tipped,
dangle the juice in front of him
but prevent him from having a sip.

For the God-forsaken womanizer
who dwelt on the sexual all of his life,
put hoards of women all around him,
let him have not even a wife.

For those who lusted for money,
put in front of them potential cash.
Let the close of every business deal
be just beyond their grasp.

Put these spirits in the real world.
Call it Purgatory or Hell.
Let them reap the pain they lavished.
Unknown to them, from life they fell.

Everyone else knows they're not real;
but to tell, the lips won't move.
Do you know that you're not one of these?
Search your soul, test, and prove! 10-8-93

35

Sweet Revenge

There's something I've been meaning to tell you,
oh precious spouse of mine;
but I thought I'd wait just a little while,
and knock out your pompous pride.
I could have told you on the way,
before you spoke to these kind folks,
telling them how that they should dress,
selling them styles of business clothes.

I could have told you when we arrived,
there was an hour before your speech;
but you seized the opportunity,
and about my style of dress you preached.

For years I've heard you carry on
about my looks, my habits, my weight.
In silence I bore your ridicule.
Inside I churned and seethed with hate.

At last here's a golden opportunity
to get some sweet revenge.
When I tell you what I need to say,
you'll sink, and hurt, and cringe.

You successfully gave your presentation.
The crowd seemed really excited.
You thought you got a good response
on the stupid jokes you recited.

Well, it's 30 seconds before your final talk
with the boss about your promotion.
About what the people seemed pleased and tickled
you haven't the slightest notion.

Roars of laughter came from the crowd
when you walked up to speak;
because there's a split down the back of your pants
and a brown stain on your briefs.

2-5-92

In Creative Writing Class I was given the
first line of this poem. I was to start from
there and continue the story in 200 words.
There's something I've been meaning
to tell you

SECTION FOUR – POEMS TO HONOR PEOPLE

An Ode to Virginia

With all your achievements you've made me so proud,
my dearest, Virginia, most precious.
Just because you are you, and you're part of me,
there are memories I'll always cherish.

I wish for your life all the delight you gave mine
with your cute little giggles and smiles.
I wish you happiness, prosperity, and joy,
and a love that will endure all the while.

Love, Dad

10-28-92

Congratulations, Ginny!!!!

This is great,
it's simply splendid,
it's a giant step,
it's a goal achieved,
it's a milestone,
it's a coming of age.

I'm so filled with pride over you
I could burst at the seams. It's
been a long, hard road from the dirty
diapers to the scholastic diploma.
But you made it! And you did a fine
job. There have been many happy times
along the way, many good things happened,
many high and lofty things accomplished.
There have also been those negative things
that make one's heart cry out with
anguish. But you weathered every storm
and came out smiling. I wish you many more
successes in life. Go forward, reach high,
don't let anything hold you back. I love
you with all my heart and I'm proud that
you're my daughter.
God bless you very much!

Your one and only Dad

5-29-93

39

The Keeper Of The Crown

This neat little box will keep your crown
from loss, mutilation, or stain;
but its worth and glory must be upheld
through many aches and pains.

Your goals are high, your accomplishments fine,
with grace you've come this far.
Your physical beauty is only surpassed
by the beauty of your heart.

In unselfish effort you use your gifts
to help those whose hopes are down.
May the works you do and the lives you touch
shine like the sparkle of the crown.

When comes the last mile, your work complete,
even the angels will be proud;
and the God of Heaven til the end of the race,
is the keeper of your crown.

6-20-93

In honor of Karmyn Tyler
    "Miss Park Cities"
based on a video presentation
of the good she does in the lives
of others, presented orally at the
time I presented her the beautiful
little box to hold her crown, when
she was competing for Miss Texas.

A Tribute to Mary Oliver

Mary Oliver stepped up onto
the burgundy-skirted stage,
like a daisy springing up
amidst crimson roses,
smiling brilliantly.
She was here to read
Her Poetry!

She was, as I expected,
intriguingly different,
yet simple as a peasant,
plain but elegant, wearing
jeans and a yellow shirt.
We're anticipating
Her Poetry!

Three shades of yellow
like the rays of the sun,
burgundy diamonds in the
background, all reflecting in
her glass of water.
She began to read
Her Poetry!

She was bent slightly by the
fullness of years, but seemed
young, and ended each poem on a
high note like there was more to come.
More to her than just
Her Poetry!

As she finished
the crowd clapped,
and the glass of water
with its many-colored
reflections became a trophy.
We loved Her Poetry!   4-16-92

41

A Tribute To The Ladies

In the smile of your face there's a touch of God's grace.
In your hug there's a bit of His love.
Your encouraging words for a heart full of fears,
bring peace from the Savior above.

The Lord works through you to do His good will
for those along your path of life.
To make flowers bloom and brighten the gloom.
You're a lovely reflection of His light.

For all that you mean to us, and all that you do,
we appreciate you more than you know.
We hope that the Lord, God from the depths of His love,
His richest blessings on you will bestow.

10-26-91

A Tribute to Kim Mallette

"I love you guys," are his final words
at the end of each Sunday's class.
A big old teddy bear, full of love and humor,
he makes each Sunday School lesson a blast.

He holds the Word of God in his heart as well as his hands.
He encourages each one in the Lord.
Knowing full well Satan's on the prowl,
he tries to equip each of us with a sword.

He is often seen in his fishing boots
without a rod or a net in his hands.
For the Lord, he has become a fisher of men,
baptizing them, into Salvation's plan.

42

Who do you know besides Kim Mallette
whose hands have been baptized numerous times?
Do you trust him to lead you in the way of the Lord?
Would you lay your heart on the line?

To you, Kim Mallette, we offer this tribute.
You'll be honored when God gets His way.
But until that day when we meet in the Heavens,
let these words be your hard-earned pay.

12-21-2002

In Honor of Dickie

Death claimed a mighty warrior.
Death stalks its prey.
This soldier fell to cancer
at forty years of age.

Upholding the banner of the King,
the Bible was his sword.
When he fell in the midst of battle
he was raised up to the Lord.

Like the Ultimate Carpenter,
woodwork was his trade.
He supervised us guys at Robert Shaw's,
took the heat for our mistakes.

He shared his life with the little guys
by coaching soccer games.
He also coached their softball,
teaching them a better way.

He was kind an good to all of us,
treated his lovely wife the same.
When he spoke a word of her,
it brought honor to her name.

It wouldn't surprise me one little bit
if when he walked into God's sight
a host of Glorious Angels chimed,
"Dickie, You'rrrre allll right!"   8-4-93

In honor of Dickie Wooldridge
who was my supervisor for a
couple years. His favorite line
was, "You'rrrre allll right!"

The Beat and the Beef

In the San Francisco Saloon that night
she sang her song Karaoke style.
Her slender form to the music swayed,
with every note she flashed a smile,
and the beat goes on.

Anxiously returning to her chair, she was
lavished with praise from her dearest friends.
With hungry eyes she examined her plate
where all that was left were bits of bread
that the beef goes on.

Stretching across the Sunflower State
the DeVore Ranch is crowded with steers.
They're second best to the Lone Star State
where the Longhorns reigned throughout the years,
and the beef goes on.

Whether we hear the beat or eat the beef
life continues with friends so dear.
The many things that we share together
make sunshine bright and Heaven near,
and the beat goes on.

The Half-Pint Hustle

My Hustle Stepper is in motion,
to the tune of the Half-Pint Hustle,
putting flexibility into my hips
and building up the muscle.

The power that makes my footsteps fly
is the strength that's from within.
With the help of many people's prayers
there's no doubt that I will win.

I'm walking in the steps of Jesus.
He makes me stronger every day.
My friends feed me spiritual spinach.
No giant can stand in my way.

If you knew from where I started,
and where I am today,
then you'd know that The Half-Pint Hustle
is the blessing for which you prayed.

11-30-98

This poem is written for and dedicated to
2-year-old McKay Crass who is receiving
therapy on her hip to correct a disability.
The Hustle Stepper is her stationary
treadmill. The Half-Pint Hustle is her
dance. She steps within the footprints of
Jesus indelibly etched on her dance floor.

A Human Angel

A human Angel passed away
in the winter of her years
and left behind a memory
that her loved ones all hold dear.

She penned many words in poetry
from an overflowing heart,
sharing God's love with those around her,
telling the richness He imparts.

Her life not only blessed her children,
the grandchildren show it too,
the things she taught by word and deed
became their souls food.

At the close of life, on her deathbed,
at the age of ninety three,
with her children all around her,
her demeanor was kind and sweet.

"Shall I ask for anything special?"
said her son preparing to pray.
"Everything's special," was the reply.
And so it was to her dying day.

With integrity she had walked the path
that Angel feet have trod.
The wrinkles she acquired in life
were all to the glory of God.

12-26-2000

In honor of Thelma Jennings
May 4, 1907 to December 13, 2000

A Little Spark is a Flame for Life

Just a little spark ignites the flame
and whoosh, the fire goes wild.
All she really meant to do
was encourage you with her smile.

But now you're stuck. You'll stay there, friend,
no matter what the weather.
So set your sights and mind on her
whenever you yearn for pleasure.

And when the bank account springs a leak
you better fill it faster.
Put the golf clubs and fishing rod back in the closet
because those things really cannot matter.

Take her to Church with you every week.
Sit right in front of the preacher.
That's the only way to soften her heart.
Then your life will be much easier.

Walk with her all your life, my friend.
Put her right beside The Savior.
You'll find that happiness and holiness
give life a better flavor.

6-9-2000

This poem was 1st written
to roast Tony & Teresa Justice
for their wedding. A couple
years later it was used to roast
Larry & Livia Jones.

Robert Shaw Carpenter

A typical Robert Shaw Carpenter
has determination on his mind.
When there's not the right tool to do the job
he has the ability to improvise.

Robert Shaw's was here serving the people,
in the days before table saws,
when the only method of making tight joints
was good men with brain and brawn.

The noble motto of every man is
"To The Work With All My Might."
Sure there're mistakes, but when we're a team
everything works out just right.

Thus we grew from a one-room shack
to the size we are today.
When we think of all the great folks we've served,
we're not in the least ashamed.

Robert Shaw furniture will be standing firm
when the last Carpenter's dead and gone.
If you want quality and deserve the best
just call Robert Shaw.

                    2-21-94

One day I caught Buck
holding a board up on
my table saw and cutting
it with a handsaw. I shot
a picture of that unusual
sight, and that prompted
this poem. His wife said
to him later, "That guy
must have had a darn good
camera to make you look
that good."

48

Hearing Hearts

Deep within the ears of our hearts
we hear your sharing voice.
Although you speak not a single word,
our hearts hear cries of joy.

In unselfish effort your fingers fly
over the lettered keys of grace.
What God has given us, through your hands,
is evident in your face.

The capturing of human words,
communication, is what we crave.
And through your unfailing fingertips
comes the wisdom that the speakers raise.

For all your faithful, dedicated work
we give you heart-felt thanks and honor;
but the greatest reward still waits for you
in the arms of our Heavenly Father.

1-11-2004

Our Yellow Rose

Like a yellow rose that's blooming in Spring
with a brilliant display of life,
there's a sparkling diamond in this group,
who shines like an Angel of light.

She came from a life of discouraging rejection,
struggling with her hearing loss.
Her heart goes out to the suffering underprivileged,
not counting the sacrifice or cost.

With dynamic personality she leads this group,
knowing how to get things done.
She never turns back no matter what the odds,
working til the victory is won.

But there is one thing that happens every year,
no matter how she yearns for a change;
on Valentines Day she turns one year older
Karen, we wish you a happy birthday!

2-14-2004

Julie

Julie, it's not time for you to leave us yet.
You are so beautiful; you are like a Wildflower,
arrayed in splendor, springing up amidst thorn bushes.
Everywhere you roam your fragrance lingers.

Our hearts would be terribly saddened to see you no more.
I prayed for you today, on just a chance that God will
hear my prayer and let it rise beyond my narcissistic heart.

If I could think such thoughts of you,
and pen these words in gentle expression of my heart,
how much more must others love you
and cherish your presence in their lives.

And wouldn't God be prone
to reach down a loving arm around you
because He wants you for His own.
He'll steady your steps and hold
you up lest you fall, and keep you here
until you're ready for Him to take you home.

When you dance with Angels
will your steps be more beautiful

than the thoughts that dance beyond this page
in the minds of those whose lives you touch.

Dear Julie, you are loved and wanted here.
The Angels can't have you yet.
God wants you to stay awhile, and
I can't think of a better reason
for you to hurry up and get well.
I miss you!
Get Well Soon

In Honor of Lois Jarvis
The Ground Zero Quilt Maker

You touched my heart today
with your wonderful work of love.
No other Angel could take your place
in our Heavenly Home above.

The reason you made this quilt
is very obvious to me.
It places loving memories
where all the world can see.

But it was Jesus working through you
to accomplish such a task.
No one in this earthly kingdom
could have designed each little patch.

When you join all those heads together
in a great starburst of grace,
each and every gazing witness
has their heart set in a blaze.

I may never get to meet you
while we walk the wounded Earth.
But you'll not escape my notice when

51

we're all joined in the big starburst.

2- 12- 2004

Shaw Christmas 1993

Twas the day before Christmas,
and all through the shop,
we were walking around talking
not doing our jobs.
The Shaw's were all aggravated,
bent out of control.
To complete Oracle by New Years
was the ultimate goal.

Wes with his cookies
and Frank's peppermints
were all that concerned us
while we dreamed of our checks.
Up with the elevator
came Robert with rage.
We all scattered quickly,
got back in our place.

Robert glanced around thoughtfully
then stormed back to his chair.
Within minutes, like thunder,
was Betty's voice on the air.

"No employee will receive a bonus,
not one little dime,
if we don't get this job out
and delivered on time."

With somber determination
we turned to the work,

thinking Robert's a scrooge,
a mean, miserly jerk.

But just like he promised
when noontime rolled around,
Pat's voice on the air
said, "Let's shut her down!"

Robert passed out the checks,
then with a smile on his face
said, "Have a nice Christmas,
and we'll see you Monday!"

12-23-93

SECTION FIVE – POEMS TO BOOST YOU OVER THE OBSTACLES OF LIFE

Just Myself

In spite of all the pain in my life,
I don't wish to be someone else.
I just want to be me, like God created me.
I love being just myself.

I walk along the new paved street
quite nearly by myself,
because with my arms around my wife
I wished she were someone else.

Ironically, that wish came true;
but it's like it was upside down,
because nothing changed about the one
I had my arms around.

It was "I" in that picture who changed.
The "I" became someone else.
And I learned no matter how I wish,
I can only change myself.

Now, I still like me just the way I am.
I don't wish to be someone else.
because in the 14 years that passed,
God made me a better self.

Now, I like you just the way you are.
I don't wish you were someone else.
Because my life is all-about me,
I give to the world, just myself.

11-11-2002

From a Whiner to a Tiger

From a whiner to a tiger,
when the transformation is complete,
there'll be nothing that can hold me back.
All my goals I will meet.

All those who seek to control me
will wither in the dust.
For their demand is my delight,
and to change my life, a must.

A challenge once embarked upon,
though to result in death may seem,
will only make me twice as strong
and fulfill my fondest dream.

Endurance is the dynamic tool
that will help me win the race,
and no matter what the circumstance,
there's no challenge I can't face.

Attitude is ninety percent
of the fuel that powers my life.
When I adopt a tiger attitude
I control my life and rights.

3-20-94

When I act like a whiner I am in victim stance. The whole worldwalks all over me. If I even set goals they seem very far out of reach. I let things happen to me because life is all chance. Well-meaning, and not so well-meaning people control me by making demands of me without knowing or caring what goes on in my life.

55

Sometimes when I undertake a challenge it so overwhelms me that I think it will surely be the death of me; but if I am able to complete the task I am twice as strong in the end and ready for the next one. If I want to be a more confident, dynamic person then to gain strength for living is the change I want. Endurance is what it takes to keep on no matter what the odds. The way I look at life is of far more importance than what the circumstances are.

Narcissism

The narcissistic personality,
as dreaded as leprosy,
everything that happens in life
is a total reflection on me.

Every look, every action,
every muffled word
is a plot to expose my guilt and shame.
Everyone's character is absurd.

Characterized by resentment and rage
the narcissist hurts inside.
He only wants to escape this world
or find something that satisfies.

Total rejection from others he gets
though he feels as important as gold.
When will those idiots come to their senses?
Their kinks and quirks he'll expose.

The way to escape narcissism is
get out of the nation called "Self."
Start doing for others. Expect no reward.
Give your time. Share your life. Offer help.

6-29-93

This too Shall Pass

This too shall pass, when time has flown,
the pain is momentary.
Release the chains and let it fall,
it's too much load to carry.

Chop the dog's tail bit by bit,
prolong the pain forever,
or make a decision and let go
a cancerous growth to sever.

To things we cling, old ideas we hold
while we try to change our lives.
Briars rip through the weakened flesh
and pierce our hearts like knives.

I quit, I give, I surrender my heart
to the One who can make it well.
I've known all along that this too shall pass.
Your loving hug will help.   8-14-94

Cognitive Reconditioning

We'll sentence you to prison and
we'll lock you up in shame; but
we'll go even further and
we'll show you how to change.

No accomplishment in the world
will be out of your range.
When you learn to change your thinking
you'll change your whole life's game.
                              4-13-93

57

Give Your Best

Every man who does his best
gives equal in terms of effort.
The one who fails to do all he can
becomes to the nation a debtor.

The one who fails to do his best,
though he does twice as much as another,
is punished for his laxity,
not rewarded for outdoing his brother.

A soldier in the heat of combat,
given a task that matched his skill,
failed to do the best he could,
though plenteous was the kill.

He was driven hard by the glorious thought
of a medal to pin on his chest;
but just because he quit too soon,
in the Earth he lies to rest.

The lust of honor impels a man
to more desperate effort expend
than the love of money or comfort;
glory stays with him in the end.

The God-given endowments of a man
fix the measure of his best.
So whether you work for money or fame,
give your worth to match the rest.

10-17-93

The idea for this poem came from a book by Edward Bellamy called "Looking Backward" from 2000 to 1887. (pg-152-154)

Inch-by-Inch It's a Cinch

Years ago when life's storms raged
I weathered them as best I could.
Like a scraggly Cedar rooted in dust,
against the gales I stood.

The wind and the rain tore at my boughs.
Needles fell to the ground.
I won the battle for stand I must,
though battered and bruised and scarred.

Then I discovered, through the wisdom of age,
that life needn't be this hard.
I had met the breeze with a one-foot ruler
and was bucking it yard by yard.

It didn't take long to change my strategy
when the simpler way I found.
I encountered a huge tornado
and into breaths I broke it down.

Now, when the challenges of life seem overwhelming
I remember with a pleasant grin
that yard by yard life's just too hard;
but inch by inch it's a cinch.

9-2-94

Sharing

Two people take an early walk
each on their own street side.
Thoughts of nature, beauty, humanness,
flow through their cluttered minds.

In America we keep us separate
from all things we do not know.
Unshared so much gets wasted.
Many experiences remain untold.

To the other's side I'll cross,
tell my story, give my name.
A friendship might be kindled
if the other does the same.

Openly communicate thoughts and feelings
once a friendship has begun;
and when things differ from heart to heart
there's no need to turn and run.

Why must we eat alone
at a table fit for four,
or turn the other way in silence,
or face the elevator door?

If we will share our empty space,
tell our stories, give a smile,
we'll shine light in deep, dark corners
making all of life worthwhile.

4-25-93

The Storm Rages

An electric storm rages in the darkened sky,
my whole being trembles and the tears flow then,
won't you hold me til my fears take flight?

Lightning rips through my anxious life,
pierces calm, squelches flickering lights, when
an electric storm rages in the darkened sky.

When pain and confusion take over my mind,
and evil the gates of my fortress bend,
won't you hold me til my fears take flight?

I am accused and sentenced before I'm tried,
punishment executed to the bitter end,
an electric storm rages in the darkened sky.

My innocence fled before my eyes.
And you, dear lady, were my one true friend.
And you held me til my fears took flight.

My bleeding heart is healed by time,
and caring concern from several friends.
An electric storm raged in the darkened sky,
but love held me til my fears took flight.

4-30-92

In a Villanelle the 1st line repeats in
the 6th, 12th, and 18th. And the 3rd
line repeats in the 9th, 15th, and 19th.
These special poems were written for
Creative Writing Class.

Trapped

Daintily, gracefully through nature's realm
the Butterfly wings its flight.
Its beautiful wing spread of black and gold
glides on the breeze like a kite.

Intricately, delicately the gold stands out
like lips that are pursed in a grin.
Two little eyelets of blue and orange
look out from the darkness within.

Without a care and never a worry
it dances from place to place,
til into the perils of danger and death
it entered my work domain.

It flit from the bench to the table saw,
then dauntless from head to head.
But, oh! rot the luck, in careless flight
it got stuck in a spider web.

It struggled and strove til strength gave out,
then collapsed, spent, in the heat.
Get up brave beauty the spider is coming,
looking for something to eat!

Because there is need, and want, and desire,
and that's how she lives day by day;
there in her beautiful state-of-the-art web
the spider sucked the life out of her prey.

Now, if you think that is the close of the story
you're sadly mistaken, my friend;
cuz that's how some precious things in this life
come to an untimely end.

Who was the last one you held trapped in your clutches,
while he poured out his heart to your needs?
And all the while his life dribbled away,
you sucked it all out with your greed.

8-1-92

Hail Storm

Hail pelts the Earth, jawbreaker size,
and dances on the lawn next door.
The wind whips and the house shakes.
Lightning rips open the sky.
Shingles fall from the roof of the house.
It thrills me, and I hope to see more.

The wind whips. Mist cools me, as I take in more.
Cars take a beating. Hail increases in size.
The roar surrounds the whole house.
I'm mesmerized as I watch at the door.
Flashes and streaks chase through the sky.
It seems like the whole Earth shakes.

The cool breeze caresses. My body shakes.
Cars move on the freeway no more.
White dots that still speckle the sky
have increased to baseball size.
Loud pops deafen. I retreat closer to the door.
Will it stop before it tears up the house?

Lights go off and on in the house.
The scared world trembles and shakes.
A fool speeds, and slides past the car next door.
He's leaving. He wants no more.
Hail increased to grapefruit size.
Destruction rages from the vicious sky.

63

Just then all changes in the vindictive sky.
Rain in torrents washes over the house
melting the hail to niggard size.
My excited body still shivers and shakes.
The threatening sky fires its missiles no more.
I am untouched in the open door.

I continue to gaze from my fortress door.
The flag waves toward the sky.
The relieved Earth trembles no more.
Calm takes over the house.
The rain stops. My body no longer shakes.
The world withstood a war this size.

Into the house, I retreat through the open door.
Only mild thunder shakes the sky
of my life, of a size I fear no more.

4-30-92

In a Sestina every sixth line
ends with a word every seventh
line must also end with. Then in
the last three lines they must all
be used again.

The Honeydew Trail

When I met you, my darling, those years ago,
your eyes like the Honeydew gleamed.
Your smile warmed every corner of my heart.
You were all that I ever dreamed.

Together we climbed to the mountaintops,
or sailed life's tempestuous sea.
You satisfied all my wants and desires.

64

You meant all the world to me.

Somewhere along the Honeydew Trail
we took a wrong curve in the street.
Your smile lost its warmth, your eyes the sparkle,
sarcasm crept into your speech.

The King and the Queen of our castle grand
became like a saint and a shrew.
Briars grew up on the Honeydew Trail
and choked out the beautiful you.

Now your eyes sparkle with a devious scheme
as you read off your Honey-do list.
You always have headaches; there is no reward,
not even as much as a kiss.

My hair is all gray now, my stature is bent,
from years of slaving for you.
I'd trade every wrinkle I've acquired in this life
for a taste of the Honeydew.

8-21-92

Dying Blossoms

In the prime of my youth I tied the knot
with a creation full of life.
Like a crape myrtle tree by a stream of water,
this beauty was my wife.

Over the years the leaves withered;
the blossoms fell to the ground.
I'd dutifully applied strong pesticide
to each little speck I found.
I looked across the bounds of the knot

to a new plant in full bloom;
but how would it flourish in the treacherous dark
of my cold heart's dull, bleak room.

My love stayed home in reality;
but in my mind rarely ceased to roam.
The frail, little crape myrtle grew briars.
Now I walk through life alone.

I'm cleaning my room and making it safe,
all the pesticide thrown away,
and I hope for a knot that will never break,
as I condition myself each day.

3-7-93

Earthen Pity Potty

I'm giving up my Pity Potty,
It doesn't work for me.
It wouldn't hold a tinkling
of love or sympathy.

It gave me a pain in the bony bottom.
It was always full of self.
It saved my stinking miseries
and stored them on a shelf.

I want one that flushes out
the junk I'm prone to treasure,
and sends it down the sewer line
with all its stress and pressure.

It clears the way for joyous thoughts
to do their healing best,
to make my heart sing out in praise,
and give it peace and rest.

I want faith as sure as gravity
to trust my Heavenly Father,
to know that He will lead the way,
and catch me when I totter.
Then I will walk as steady as iron
that doesn't sway or bend,
that endures the heat of the fiery furnace,
then is poured out to its end.

It's lifted up as a cast-iron vessel,
and used for whatever the smith desires.
It's much stronger than this earthen pot,
and for its purpose never tires.

12-31-2003

Coping With Life

When something is broken in my hectic life
I trust the strength of Super Glue.
When all my skies seem dark and cloudy
Visine will make them blue.

When everything seems to be all in a jam
there's K-plex Traffic in the air.
When all around is sinking sand
I call Ram Jack Foundation Repair.

I call Roto Rooter Drain Cleaning Service
when things don't flow so smooth.
When I think my spirits are lifted too high
I watch the channel five evening news.

When I want what I can't find anywhere else
I do a Sam's Wholesale Warehouse check.
When I need specific area guidance
I get a map of the Metroplex.
When I long for something better than this
I get a piece of the Prudential Rock.
When you feel you just can't cope with life
there's help for you round the clock.

3-10-93

Ridicule

A hair-lipped fellow, to compound his troubles,
developed a serious problem with stutter.
Said he, with difficulty, to his impatient friends,

68

"Iiiee gggoo ttoue rrruneyh ffforeh ggovnerh."
(I'm going to run for governor).

They scoffed and sneered, and rejected the jerk.
To nothing would amount such a nerd.
With patience he bore all their ridicule,
never uttered a reviling word.

He took Voice Diction at TCJC,
Assertiveness Training with Deborah Moore.
He took the Governor seat away from Ann Richards
in nineteen ninety and four.

He influenced the House to pass a resolution
prohibiting ridicule in a public place.
Some months later six "crazy people"
achieved prominence in the human race.

One revolutionized criminal justice
using hypnotism to alter the brain.
Two promoted regular space travel
with a nuclear powered astroplane.

One wipes out most of the serious addictions
using compulso-rhythmic monitoring.
Two drastically reduced the rate of suicide
teaching love and kindness and honoring.
As for those ones who did all the scoffing,
well, they get along okay.
Two work sanitation for the city of Dallas.
Three clean along the highway.

3-8-93

69

The Bad Breath Epidemic

The air is putrid,
talk is light,
nostrils offended,
lips held tight.
There's a bad breath epidemic raging through the land
and nothing is being helped by smokers on every hand.

Some have dog-breath,
others have spice,
some have death-breath,
some vile and vice.
There's a bad breath epidemic raging through the land
intensified by cokes, coffee, or beer scouring the glands.

The preacher sends his
out over the pews,
the worker thickens the air
like the paper mills do.
There's a bad breath epidemic raging through the land
and like a plague it's getting out of hand.

If you'll use Close-Up
and brush your fangs
you'll save the population
from harsh nasal pains.
There's a bad breath epidemic raging through the land,
and I'm told if I clean my mustache it wouldn't smell so bad.

5-8-92

This poem was written in honor of
the guys at work, because sometimes
the air gets pretty thick and hairy
around there. Since I'm hearing-
impaired, I read lips; but sometimes
I want to read them from a distance
through a pair of binoculars.

The Perfect Woman

Women do have their faults,
but they are the ultimate creation,
as was Galatea,
before her incarnation.

Pygmalion, the woman hater,
with wantonness possessed,
created the ultimate woman,
untouched by all the rest.

He shaped her from sculpted stone
and passion filled his heart,
but he was stricken with deep sadness,
she was only a work of art.

He kissed her and held her,
her cold, passive form caressed.
He cried to the Goddess of Passionate Love
in his hopeless wretchedness.

Venus heard his plea and gave the word,
Galatea melted in his arms.
They were married and had a son,
but was theirs a life of charms?

Women have their faults, you know,
but then, so do men.
Not one is totally perfect, but
there's perfection in all of them.
Galatea had a heart of stone,
which was, of course, made flesh,
but every little corner???
What would be your guess???

4-14-92

71

Based on the story,
Pygmalion and Galatea
by Edith Hamilton
in Legends of Long Ago
Crowell- Collier
Publishing Co. 1962

In Charge

I hope you all appreciate
our elders strong and wise;
if someone else were put in charge
we all might be surprised.

Last night I chanced to contemplate
a switching of Church-staff;
putting Monica Pope in charge
we'll all get a good laugh.

John Bizzell became Building Manager,
Bill Werner- Minister of the Preaching,
Marguerite Thompson was Office Secretary,
Betty Leggett- Minister of Outreaching.

Her own dear husband took her job
as child's education planner,
the song leader was Tim Shoulders,
Minister of youth was Eddie Tanner.

Then just for double fun
in charge I put Eddie Tanner,
Betty Leggett became the preacher,
John Bizzell- Child's Education Planner.
The Song Leader was Marguerite Thompson,
Minister of Youth was Monica Pope,
The rest I'll let you guess,
as you can see there's not much hope.

72

To straighten out this mixed up mess
put Marguerite Thompson in charge,
all faces take their place again
and the work here carries on.

I think that we should keep our elders
though some mistakes they make,
and honor their decisions,
and keep God's gifted in their place.

But if you chance to change your mind
want someone else in the lead,
just turn The Church Staff Wheel.
Possibilities are numerous indeed.

Just for fun at the Meadowbrook Church of Christ I took
the pictures of the church leaders as they were arranged in
the directory and pasted them onto a paper plate. I placed
a movable dial over the picture plate that put each leader's
title under their picture. When you chanced to turn the
dial putting an alternate leader "in charge" it would
reorganize the whole church staff.

A Sympathizing Tear
1-18-92

One
li'l
tear
drop
from
watery
eyes comes
trickling down
the face. Wet and
clear it slips to the
lips leaving a salt trail
in its place. One little drop
but a story it tells bringing
sympathy from a friend.Squeeze
me and hug me & tell me you
love me, til all of the
tear drops end.

Our Ring and My Tears

I loved the Darling Companion of my youth,
though I failed to express it in so many ways.
I wanted us to be together
for all of our earthly days.
We've been separated a long, long time,
so many tears I've shed.
The farthest distance ever between us
74

was the width of our king-sized be
I hang our ring on my teardrops
in honor of my long-time friend.
May each of us find fulfillment in life
with the hope of a victorious end.

The Love of Script

Scriptophilia, an undying love for writing,
cries from a craving heart for a description of beauty,
righteousness, and love. As a prescription for festering,
incurably cancerous attitude, powerful Scripture pierces like
peroxide. It is postscript of the Great Physician's message
tattooed as an inscription on the heart.

Other manuscripts flow with beauty, inspire to greatness,
powerfully evoke anger – laughter – lust. Life's subscription
holds pleasures, pains, and passions told in proscription.

In the transcription of the author's thoughts we sometimes
learn of one's ascription to and passion for a style of life.

In all of script can you detect, that which you love best?

All hail the power of the written word, scriptophilia cries
again!

4-7-92

An Artist by Heart

The true carpenter is an artist by heart,
shaping and fabricating a magnificent creation.
Nature's intricately figured grain formation
is made a masterpiece by the worker of art.

First, it is dull gray wood with gnarled bark,
then a genius plan and steps of construction.
Yes, the true carpenter is an artist by heart,
shaping and fabricating a magnificent creation.

Sure hands shape what he designs from his heart.
Beauty caresses it lovingly. Delightful sensations
fill an observer's eyes. Skillful manipulation
of each piece, precisely formed and assigned a part,
the true carpenter is an artist by heart.

3-23-92

In a Rondel the first line must
be repeated in the seventh and
the thirteenth.

Little Boxes

There's a workshop in Keller
that makes these little boxes.
They are decorative. They are beautiful.
And they're all made just the same.

There is Walnut and Mahogany,
Pecan and Brazilian Rosewood.
And they're all made from bits and pieces.
And they're all made with lots of love.
People use them for the purpose
of containing precious property.

They hold jewelry, stamps, and flowers,
cards, and candy, and other things.

There are people in Fort Worth, Texas
who don't know what they're missing
until they've purchased little boxes
by The Carpenter's Workshop.

If you're wondering where to get some
visit The Carpenter's Workshop
In Keller, Texas in Tarrant County
Where Blackwood Drive meets Florence Road.

written 8-9-94
revised 2-24 2004

What Is It?

It's whatever the mind can conceive
early in the morning on a snowy day.
It could be a display of men's wedding rings,
or a hundred roll bugs at play.

It could be the result of a twist bit through metal
laid neatly all in a row.
Or it could be the wild confusion of the mind
from a late night TV show.

It's whatever you choose to make it today
from the depths of your creative mind.
But don't look too long or think too hard
or you may chance to become blind.
Today is the day to think about love

and pass it on to a precious heart;
so get that thing out of my monitor
I'm not feeling all that smart.

2-14-2004

On Valentines Day a friend
forwarded me a picture
through the e-mail with these
words at the top: "What is it?"
This poem is an answer to that.

SECTION EIGHT - CARESSING THE DETAIL

The Carpenter

Into the room walked the carpenter.
The windblown look of his hair running
pell mell, helter skelter, and curly all over
was a whole lot kinky.
There was an almost sideways smile,
a wistful grin, on his face as he considered
how he must surely look in the eyes of his friends.

He was a slender figure silhouetted against
the rays of the morning sun. The tint of
his hair glistening in the light was
shining as bright as his big red
mustache.

The Lady

Looking across the room,
our eyes met in a moment of pure delight.
Her face was almost haggard from years of
hardship, struggle, and worry.

Bedraggled and worn she looked like
she'd been drug through the mill.
The Spirit of God that had always been
evident in her face, seemed to be missing.

Her eyes brightened in recognition
And she smiled warmly. Then I knew
She was still my beautiful friend
Kimi Lee Taylor.

Vicarious Voices

Hilarious and intriguing are the voices I hear
with this malfunction of my ears.
Hi-pitched voices sound like
The Chipmunks, and low voices
sound hair-lipped and nasal.

Both are distorted and garbled as if
they were being channeled through
a static filled radio. They both have
that silly "Elmer Fudd Pucker" style.

A Kiss of Ice

Like a cool stream from a huge air-conditioner
the cold wind buffets my chin.
It slips through the minuscule opening
around the face shield, as I ride my
motorcycle to work on a forty degree morning.
Relentlessly the icy breeze kisses my chin.
Penetrating to the bone and permeating through
scores of cells and tissue it reaches
its ultimate destination; and I arrive at
the shop brain dead.

A Touch

As my hand sinks into the billowy softness,
the heat that engulfs it is almost unbearable.
The feel is silky smooth, but the splits and cuts
on my fingers begin to sting and burn
as if being invaded by an army of fire ants.

It feels slippery, slimy, and a little bit grimy
as my thumb rubs the cuts on my fingertips.
Deeper and deeper into the heat I plunge
my hand. At last I feel the hard, spherical
shape at the bottom. One small jerk and then
like the roar of the river-falls
my dishwater is sucked down the drain.

A Taste

The taste is very sweet, like the lips of a beautiful lady,
as I sink my teeth into this mound of delightful
temptation. At first it is hard, but not at all crunchy.
As my jaws close, very quickly it bursts into
bits of rich and delicious goodness.

It melts and spreads over the roof of my mouth
causing a squeal of delight as the first of it
hits the throat and slides past my tonsils.
Running my tongue over my teeth,
I get the last of the smooth and luscious sweetness.
With one quick swallow, down into the deep
cavern of darkness my chocolate kiss
disappears forever.

A Single Sentence

Sometimes, even in the midst of all the emotional pain
of my most serious and destructive dysfunctions caused
by a lifetime of spiritually incorrect thinking, my mind
becomes so clear and the short-term memory so extensive
and inexhaustible that I can create and retain some of the
longest, most interesting and complex, yet easily readable
sentences, which if interpreted correctly by even the simplest
minded reader, demonstrate a profound ingenuity in this
writer that is rarely found in even the most brilliant minds
of the ones who are considered to be well above average in
their ability to enunciate a verbal response using their choice
of the once believed to be well over six hundred thousand
good and wholesome words of our English language today
with all of its many wonderful adjectives that can be used in
place of profanity, as some would tend to lean toward when
in a bind to give a good description of what they are feeling
at any given moment, as in the example where I was telling a
friend just today that if I was called upon to fight for any
cause I would endeavor to campaign for further women's
liberation in all things, including romance and love affairs, so
that the man would not have to have the responsibility of
making his intentions known, if by reading all the signs he
decided she was interested and wanted to ask her out,
because if he was wrong her wrath would come down on him
like an angry wolf on the innocent fold, and make him feel
much smaller than a little bitty fire ant in the enormous
Grand Canyon, thereby causing him all the embarrassment
and pain of being rejected and put back in his place, which
at first was down amongst the grains of sand on the beach
of his disreputable and unremarkable life, a cause for which
I really believe, if my efforts proved to be fruitful, that I
would undoubtedly be greatly rewarded since I am single and
free.

3-31-92 338 words
82

Like a Little Jesus

Your heart is totally given to God.
It stands porter on your mind.
You're blessed with Him in the grace of
giving encouragement to the spiritually blind.

Your words have a way of turning on the light.
To the "Love of Jesus" they give birth.
If everyone would think a little more like you,
God's will, would be done on Earth.

When a friend is struggling you're there to help,
giving him that for which he has need.
To the extent you've done it to the least of
these, Jesus said, you've done it unto me.

You never take part in malicious gossip.
You stand porter on your mind.
Your thoughts give healing where it is needed,
to the hurting, the lame, and the blind.

Your reward is great in The Kingdom of Heaven.
The Father & Son say you have pleased us.
Many of us are a little like Jesus,
but you-are like A Little Jesus.

2-26-2004

SECTION NINE - MORE RECENT POEMS

A Tiny Child

A tiny child is a spark of life
kindled aflame by the breath of God,
fearfully and wonderfully woven together,
with a gospel of love its feet are shod.

Kaycee breezed in to Earth in the heat of July
setting wilted flowers abloom,
and found her place in the family of five,
her sisters more than happy to give her room.

It remains to be seen what the Lord makes of her,
what her talents turn out to be;
but for now she's exploring the mysteries of Earth,
and making relatives smile with glee.

The greatest blessing she's found so far
is the faith of her mother and dad.
She knows they honor God who created her;
and her life will never turn out bad.

So this family of five walks the earth in love,
sharing their joy with all whom they see.
There are plans God has in store for them,
And whatever will be, will be.

8-14-2010

All For Your Hug

I'd just like you to know, my Special Friend,
what I would do your hug to receive.
You'll find me going to very great lengths.
You are extremely important to me.

To experience your love I'd walk barefoot
on a rough gravel road for a mile
with my hopes set on nothing more than a hug
and your beautiful, captivating smile.

To be sure our friendship is still intact
I'd swim the great ocean, battle the sea,
climb a tall iceberg, and cross a fiery pit
in hopes that I'd find you smiling at me.

And if you have any troubles, feel any pain,
find that you have tribulations to bare,
don't hesitate for a second to call on me;
know assuredly that I am someone who cares.

This is only to tell you, my Special Friend,
I want you to know and fully believe
beyond any doubt, without any fear
that you mean more than the world to me.

7-18-2006

To my Special Friend, _____,
Friends only forever, from ____

A True Love   11-01-09

When life is like your bath water
swirling down the drain,
not slowing down for anything
until you reach the resting place;

along the way you miss true love
when it isn't keeping up the pace,
accept those speeding just like you,
and get tangled in the race.

But an older man is far wiser.
He lives like a slower tune,
enjoying beautiful things before him,
and one of them is you.

He never misses a chance to tell
of the wonders under the blue,
and won't pass up a chance to bless
the one whose arms he steps into.

True love knows no age limits.
Pure intimacy knows no shame.
Let observers looking in be jealous
cause they can't play your game.

His offspring are his equals,
no longer treated as children.
They rock to the tune of life,
in the spiritual realm they are pilgrims.

Perhaps some surprising things
will surface in their time;
but they will be your wonders.
Don't let them blow your mind.
Boaz didn't care how young she was

when he decided to love his girl;
and he didn't let her precious youth
make his whiskers curl.

When she's past the age of majority,
she makes her own decisions.
Most impressive is her intelligence,
and for her life, her visions.

Ruth didn't care how old he was
when she decided to love her guy.
Don't let age difference bother you,
or lost years make you cry.

Just decide to enjoy the love,
and years you'll share together.
Be his girl, his darling dear,
and make your life a pleasure.

Doves of Peace

Doves are roosting in an old oak tree
unafraid of winter's bite.
Catching last rays of a fading sun.
It appears they're parked there for the night.

Next door earlier the little birds fed,
raking out of the feeders a generous store,
covering the ground with abundant seed;
the Doves ate hungrily and wanted no more.

Now light is fading from December's Earth.
The Doves are the color of the leafless limb.
Silhouetted conspicuously against a light blue sky,
 resting in perfect peace, lazily they primp.
The little birds have all disappeared.
With the coming of dusk, where do they go?

87

In early morning they will return,
feeders will swing to a melodious tone.

Life is all around me, peace perfect peace.
I have no more care than the Doves.
God is controlling the passing of time.
Day's deeds are done in the essence of love.

12-26-2006

From a Daniel to a Michael

From a Daniel to a Michael,
when the transformation is complete,
there'll be nothing that can hold her back;
all of God's Angels she will meet.

She'll remember no more her lonely past,
or any injustices she endured;
since she honored God with her life over time
anything that was lacking He has cured.

Though Daniel was a man of God
established in all His ways,
Michael is the chiefest of Angels,
rendering service for the saints.

It came about in the course of time
that Kevin & Beverly tied the knot.
From McDaniel to Madam Michael
her move was one step up.

May their relationship grow and bloom in the Lord.
May they plant flowers in the hearts of many.
May they enshrine each other in a rainbow of love,
and live in the abundance of spiritual plenty.

5-21-2009

God's Wonders in my Life   2-9-2010

Oh, give me a chance to toot my own horn, and
I'll tell of God's wonders from the day I was born.
Before I knew Him in the days of my youth
He was always my protection, and Him I will choose.

When I was age five, from a bear on the trail,
He through my mother rescued us without fail.
In that same year, a Copperhead snake did
us-kids no harm in the old car where we played.

When I was age ten, I threw a can of gas in the fire.
The woodstove roared like a rocket taking flight.
Later that year, a huge Rattler across the trail,
me with my hatchet missed coming into his sight.

At ten years old when my dad broke my back,
God helped me through every bout of abuse.
At age twelve I lay exhausted in the snow,
my hands and feet froze but I didn't lose their use.

At age sixteen God provided a way of escape
from two men bent on the performance of rape.
And that year I got sick on Friendship Mound,
guzzling a beer from an old Antique Shop.

At age sixteen I fell asleep at the wheel.
Woke up to honking horns and tires' squeal.
Rolled a dunebuggy down an embankment steep,
I landed, then the buggy landed next to my cheek.

At age twenty skiing on Benbrook Lake, I literally
turned sideways to miss sliding into a snake.
Barely calmed down, I saw another on the trailer
shortly after we pulled the boat from the lake.

89

At age twenty-one in an abandoned old house
got knocked off my feet cutting a 220 volt wire.
Many times over the years I withstood the zap
when the positive and negative arced and spit fire.

At age twenty-three sleeping drunk in the ditch,
my sweet wife towed me and the dune buggy in.
At age twenty-four, in trouble, on a drunken spree,
I promised to drink no more, when God rescued me.

Then it came time to give my life to God
and with the Gospel of Peace my feet were shod.
And all that He said in the scriptures I heeded,
in times of trouble He gave the solution I needed.

My broken back during worship He healed, and
I had a fun, active life with my kids and my wife.
At age twenty-five on our wooded ten acres, I
stepped next to a Water Moccasin coiled to strike.

Financial blessings, family blessings, chances to serve,
Bible studies, sharing times, and spiritual growth;
but because of emotional immaturity
my married life came to a close.

At age thirty-three saved from self-destruction,
He set my life on a much higher plane.
He gave admonitions and instructions in dreams.
At times He gave healing and removal of pain.

At age thirty-nine in a motorcycle accident, I flew
twenty feet through the air, landed clear of the crash.
In 94 with bad credit I purchased a $10,000.00 car,
paying it off with God's plan was like paying cash.
Since it came from God, He saved it from damage.
It got sideswiped once and He erased the scratch.
Once sliding down a steep ice-covered hill,

stopped at the bottom within inches of the crash.
At age forty-one I survived a very harsh beating.
Why it happened I haven't a clue.
The next day during the Lord's Supper
I was reminded that Jesus experienced that too.

On February 10th of 98, all I did was change my mind,
to relinquish fear and focus on love,
MS went into remission for two long years,
and my life took pattern after things above.

August 1st of 98 began the first of seven 40-day fasts.
For thousands of people my girlfriend and I prayed.
We drew close to God with all of our might.
I read the Bible through, thirty chapters a day.

At age twenty-four God gave me memory techniques.
At 41 He led me to memorize scripture and history.
I did dramatic presentations to bless His people.
He made my life an adventure of doing good deeds.

At age forty-five He healed a gash under my eye,
through the hands of the girl I wanted for my bride.
From age thirty-three to fifty-four He spoke many times
in 3am conversations or visions of the night.

At age forty-eight I was blessed with early retirement.
With Multiple Sclerosis I had been struggling for years.
From the waist down I'd been paralyzed twice.
And at age thirty-seven it had deafened my ears.

God gave me back all the time I gave Him,
rest from my labors and plenty of income,
a chance to do things hard to find time for,
and a more intimate walk with the Lord.
At age forty-eight when I fell from a two-story roof,
I was eased to the ground with no injuries.

For three and a half years in a search for my twin,
He performed many miracles and blessings for me.

We reunited after my search, at age forty-nine,
she and I had been separated since age thirteen.
Seven years after I began the long search,
she was reunited with our family at age fifty-three.

At age forty-nine while visiting a friend,
I got stung on the mustache by two-dozen bees.
It sent Multiple Sclerosis into deep remission.
At age fifty-four I'm still virtually MS free.

At age fifty-two God rescued my son
who hanging himself tried to take his life.
A miracle of timing, and with my broken wrists,
to cut the ropes, I barely handled the knife.

There were many more miracles throughout my life,
and the biggest one is that I'm still here.
I didn't even mention that at age sixteen
a speeding bullet zinged past my ear.

Today at age fifty-four I finished reading the Bible,
completely through in forty days for the 17th time.
It's the most worthwhile thing I've ever done,
I wouldn't trade it for honors given to spiritual giants.

For nothing that I myself have done,
but only through Jesus can my salvation be.
I have run the race. I have kept the faith.
The crown of life is waiting for me.

List of Miracles

Bear on the garden trail – age 5
Copperhead in the car – age 5
Gasoline in the fire – age 10
Huge Rattler across the trail – age 10
Broken back – age 10
Abuse many times – age 4-17
Exhausted in the snow – age 12
Frozen hands and feet – age 12
Way of escape from the homos – age 16
Sick on Friendship Mound – age 16
Asleep at the wheel – age 16
Rolled the dune buggy – age 17
Skiing into a Water Moccasin – age 20
Water Moccasin on the boat trailer – age 20
Electrical explosion – age 21
Electrical shocks many times – age 19-39
Sleeping in the ditch – age 23
Rescued from drunken trouble – age 24
Redemption – age 24
Solutions when needed – age 24-54
Healing of the broken back – age 25
Cotton Mouth Water Moccasin next to my leg – age 25
Financial blessings – age 24-54
Saved from self-destruction – age 33
Admonitions – age 24-54
Removal of pain – age 33-54
Motorcycle accident – age 39
Purchased a car with bad credit – age 39
Saved from auto damage – age 40
Erased the side-swipe – age 40
Survived a battering – age 41
Remissions of Multiple Sclerosis – ages 44 & 49
Fasting and Bible reading – age 43-54
Memorizing long documents – age 40-54
Healed a gash under my eye – age 45

Conversations in the night – 48-54
Visions of the night – 33-54
Early retirement – age 48
Paralysis only temporary – age 48
Involuntary bee sting therapy – age 49
Finding my twin sister after 37 years – age 50
Rescued my son from suicide – age 52
Surgery without pain – age 54
Many other blessings – all my life

Happy Anniversary!

I hope it's been a lot of years
you've held hands and hearts together.
Cherish every ounce of sweetness,
you deserve life's one best pleasure.

Together walk the King's highway
and leave your cares behind.
Look at anything that would distract
as if your eyes were blind.

This next year will be another lap
around the concourse of romance.
Tonight's the time to catch your breath
and continue the rhythm of the dance.

The only thing I can't figure,
though my thoughts be in a whirl,
how your darling companion came to be
the luckiest man in the world!
Oct. 25, 2005

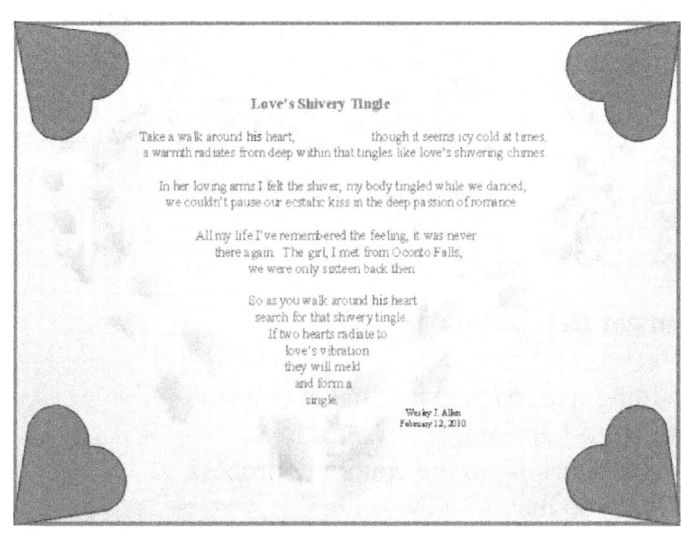

Love's Shivery Tingle

Take a walk around his heart,   though it seems icy cold at times,
a warmth radiates from deep within that tingles like love's shivering chimes

In her loving arms I felt the shiver, my body tingled while we danced;
we couldn't pause our ecstatic kiss in the deep passion of romance

All my life I've remembered the feeling, it was never
there again. The girl, I met from Oconto Falls,
we were only sixteen back then

So as you walk around his heart
search for that shivery tingle.
If two hearts radiate to
love's vibration
they will meld
and form a
single.

Wesley J. Allen
February 12, 2010

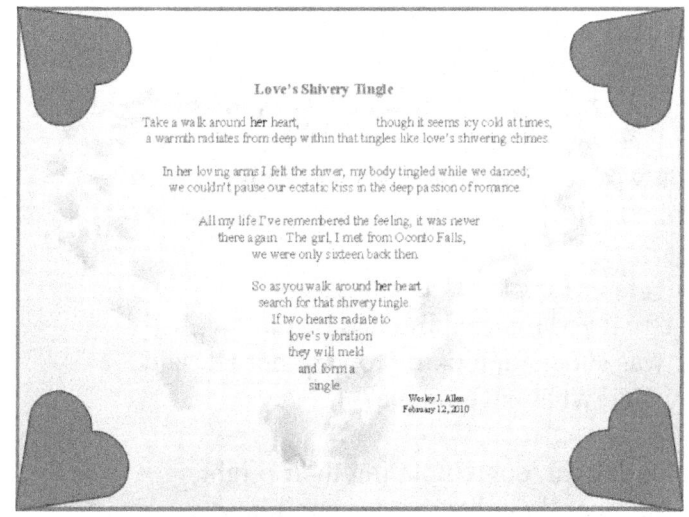

Love's Shivery Tingle

Take a walk around her heart,   though it seems icy cold at times,
a warmth radiates from deep within that tingles like love's shivering chimes

In her loving arms I felt the shiver, my body tingled while we danced;
we couldn't pause our ecstatic kiss in the deep passion of romance

All my life I've remembered the feeling, it was never
there again. The girl, I met from Oconto Falls,
we were only sixteen back then

So as you walk around her heart
search for that shivery tingle.
If two hearts radiate to
love's vibration
they will meld
and form a
single.

Wesley J. Allen
February 12, 2010

95

Moments of Realization

The wedding had reached its final conclusion
at the moment I arrived.
The preacher turning to the couple in process
said, "Now you may kiss the bride."

Sometimes facial expressions speak volumes.
They arrive at nearer the truth.
Some are so extraordinarily delightful
they give life a delicious boost.

"Are we're really married now?" His expression said;
and his face was filled with zeal.
Her look was smug as if under her breath
She said, "I told you this is for real."

Moments later I captured an expression,
when he realized married life had begun,
as if he was shocked, looking toward her He said,
"Oh my God what have I done?"

In gleeful delight, contemplating their plight,
        with her thoughts that we can't hear,
so calm and resolute in her thinking Her look said,
"You'll get used to it, Dear."

11-24-2004

Inna's Poems
My Darling
My Darling is a lovely lady,
my fabulous grand prize.
Her beauty stands out majestically;
love deepens her clear blue eyes.

She knows it doesn't take bare skin
to attract a fine and real man.
She's modest and she's precious.
For decency she takes her stand.

We will grow in love together,
Never falling as many will claim.
If you fall in love, you've lost your footing.
The relationship may end in shame.

My Darling is across the ocean,
sleeping soundly while I write.
She may read this while I sleep,
dreaming of my Angel in the night.

I adjure you by the stars of heaven
and by everything that's right,
don't waken my Darling until she pleases.
She's dreaming of her Angel in the night.

It may not be the right time yet
to tell her that I love her.
How can I not love this sweet and precious girl?
And now with all my thoughts a stir,

I'll whisper in her ear.
My Darling, Inna, I love you.
Be my Darling Companion, Inna.
With all my heart I love you.

Wes 10-8-07 10:00pm

97

A Beautiful Land

I know of a land well up into the clouds
where beautiful mansions exist.
The sun's rays beam on doors of glass
enhancing beautiful steps of onyx.

Though it's a marvelous place much like Heaven,
it's not where our King abides.
But it's a place to go to escape the earth
where we from our troubles can hide.

Come with me there, my beautiful friend,
into this land of love
where we float on clouds amidst splendid beauty,
and sing as sweet as pure white doves.

From right where we are we can travel today
into this land so fair.
Because only in thought, deep in our minds,
can we ever enter there.

Your loving words will fuel my jet,
and mine will give rise to your heart.
And we'll meet in that land everyday every night,
where nothing can cause us to part.

Let's begin every morning by expressing our love
hold each other in thoughts and charms;
in the evening relax and share our dreams,
planning our rendezvous in each others arms.

by Wesley J. Allen
October 19, 2007

98

My Decision

I've settled into the joy of relationship,
my heart is with love aflame.
There's no girl in the world I'd rather be with
than this exciting and lovely young dame.

She's dreamt of a time for so many years
when she'd meet her handsome prince.
And our hearts are bonding in perfect unison.
We were both kept for a time such as this.

Now it remains to take those first steps,
we're meeting at Christmas time.
Into the New Year we'll walk together in love,
our hearts melded with the tie that binds.

No relationship is ever perfect
but we'll work at it with all of our hearts;
it is my hope that we'll always be together
until the end of our lives do us part.

by Wesley J. Allen
October 20, 2007

Do You Think

Do you think there
could possibly be
someone else for you
or another for me?

I love every inch of
your beautiful face.
I love the wonders of
your style and grace.

There's no other girl
on Elena's site
who could turn my head
or my eyes delight.

You are the one for me, Inna.
You make my heart soar through the clouds.
You are the Dream Mate for me, Darling.
You are dispelling all of my doubts.

by Wesley J. Allen
October 21, 2007

Thoughts of You

You fill my thoughts both day and night.
Your love to me is a pot of gold.
Your beauty in my eyes surpasses all.
Without your arms around me I am so cold.

Your words to me are as precious as silver.
Your wish is my only command.
When we shall meet it will be like Heaven.
We'll sing together in an Angel band.

Inna My Love

Two o'clock in the afternoon
is the perfect time to write.
To me you'll say Good Morning
and to you I'll say Good Night.

There is no girl so precious to me
as the one behind your smile.
For you I know even without my shoes,
I'd walk five thousand miles.

I know you love me, Inna,
but please don't cease to tell,
if you call me all those special names
I'll stand right up and yell.

INNA, I LOVE YOU SO MUCH!
You're the Darling Companion for me.
You're romantic, you're exciting, you're
the one with whom my heart is pleased.
Inna, I have lots of friends
but all pale in comparison to you.
You're my one and only Love,
For you I'll do whatever I have to do.

by Wesley J. Allen
October 24, 2007

We Have Love

Your love is tremendous,
your heart is like gold.
Its value and its warmth
have precious beauty untold.

Take your time getting to know me
and you will never let go.
Your happiness turned to bliss
Is only just down the road.

Understanding and love
is all that it takes
to communicate with each other
and what happiness it makes!

Love's Blaze
My love is a blazing fire
that will not scorch or burn.
It will only warm your very soul,
comfort you at every twist and turn.

It will set your precious heart ablaze,
just like mine is now,
all because of your loving words,
you'll float with me on the clouds.

My love is a power to light your fire,
make you feel light hearted and free.
You will dance from place to place
you'll be as joyous as you can be.
 I pledge to you my love Dear Inna
in a way that's pure and nice.
And when I meet you face to face
it will be the happiest moment of our lives.
Wesley J. Allen
October 29, 2007

Words of Love

No other girl can be so blessed
as the one to whom I write.
My prolific words of beauty and love
are like star shine in the night.

Feelings and thoughts break forth in rhyme
and change celestial motion,
as in my heart her wonderful love
is causing tremendous commotion.

To the Postal Carrier   10-15-07
Postal carrier, hard-working and kind,
handle this package in any way that you wish.
It's only a blanket to keep my Sweetheart warm.
Winters are cold in Belarus, at Minsk.

It can't be damaged in any respect
unless you meet with flood or hurricane;
or if perchance it is torn to shreds
when a vicious dog gets out of his place.
 Deliver it safe and you'll bless my Honey.
She needs it a lot more than any other gift.
And you for your kindness will receive a reward.
The Great Angel knows, and all treasures are His.
 You are a treasure to us, God bless
you for all that you do!

Dear Wes this is your poem? Thank you.
 I love you.

The Dance of Life
My heart longs to see you.
I think about you very much.
I want to hold you in my arms
and feel your loving touch.

I'll whirl you in the dance of life
and gracefully show my charm.
I'll kindly show you every step,
waltz together arm in arm.

If ever your feelings are hurt
I'll mend them with a kiss.
I'll give my everything for you;
your old life you'll never miss.

I've Got a Sweetheart

I've got a Sweetheart, way over the ocean
in a distant land far beyond the sea.
Everyday my Sweetheart sends me her love and
shares her warm heart when she writes to me.

I love her dearly, there's no one like her,
she's smart, and pretty; she's a loving Doll.
I'll cross that ocean just to meet her.
I'll find her the best way that I know how.

We'll be together at Christmas time
when the city is decked out in pretty lights.
Of all the splendor in that big city
she's the most brilliant beautiful sight.

Our hearts will meet and both be raptured,
with blazing love, wonder powers ignite.
The spark of love will ignite a huge flame
more brilliant than all the city lights.
 I've got a Sweetheart, way over the ocean
in a distant land far beyond the sea.
Everyday my Sweetheart sends me her love and
shares her warm heart when she writes to me.

by Wesley J. Allen
November 5, 2007

Russian Scam

Wes: Hello, My Beautiful Russian Scam:
Warm and loving are all my thoughts of you.
I love the way you're treating me.
I'm pleased with everything you say and do.

Inna: Hello, My Handsome American Victim:
Your words just warm my heart.
You're a master of the English language.
And you're also very smart.

Wes: I cherish the day I found your name
on the famous Elena's Models site.
Your wonderful face captivated my eyes.
Now your words brighten deep dark nights.

Both: Together we'll walk the snow-covered streets
in Minsk, Belarus at Christmas time.
Later we'll walk, along the lake, in
Grapevine, Texas during summertime.

Inna: But don't forget, My Precious American Victim,
I am only after your money.
It wouldn't be right for a smart man like you
to become a devious Scammer's Honey.

Both: Oh, glorious day on the Internet,
the first time you said, "I love you."
There was never another in Cyberspace
who excites me as much as you do.

Wes: Remember, My Fabulous Russian Scam,
I'm wary of your devious tactics.
I take all the wisdom I've gained on the Web
and put it into everyday practice.

Inna: Yes, My Darling American Victim,
I've seen your high intelligence.
You only detected the Scammer's plot
cuz my words weren't sharp or elegant.

Both: I dream of the time when we'll be together,
the Scammer and the Victim,
he'll stay out, and work in the shop,
and she'll stay in the kitchen.

Wes: I love to be your Victim, My Darling,
and you'll always be My Scam.
Both: Mix into intimacy what we've learned of each other
and we'll share it all like Spam.

Inna & Wes   Our Email Courtship
First expression of interest & note 9-29-07 by Inna

After expressions of interest, Response 10-5-07 by Wes

First "I love you" in a poem by Wes 10-9-07

After expressions of love, First "I love you" by Inna 10-19-07
First International phone conversation 10-27-07

Purchase airline tickets to meet 11-2-07 by Wes
Together for Christmas and New Years

Writing to
each other
≈ 250 pages
in October.

The Night after Christmas-Tall Tale   12-3-2008

Twas the night after Christmas in the snow-covered north;
Grandma and Grandpa were sitting out on the porch.
They were thinking about family much smarter than they,
having good conversation around the warm fireplace.

Gram with her sniffles, and Pap with lips chapped
were singing and laughing as if they were cracked.
When just across the yard they heard a great roar,
climbing over each other in hopes to see more.

The porch swing tipped over dumping Pap on his pouch,
and all Gram could see was the kids on the couch.
They looked so nice and warm, there inside the house,
while behind her that roar was getting tremendously loud.

Just then it happened in wonder and surprise,
the earth opened its mouth right before their eyes.
This wasn't an earthquake or volcano or such,
for the soil stacking up was infinitely much.

The neighbor, for Christmas, got a brand new backhoe,
and when he finally got it started, it really let go.
Digging a furrow it sped across five acres,
then whirling like an auger it descended Earth's layers.

It churned and roared in an ear-splitting sound,
and passed through the earth going straight down.
It kicked out the soil like gophers building a home,
creating a hill as high as the mountains in Rome.

It wasn't for naught that the hill had been made.
It became a ski slope for folks of every age.
And all during that winter the whole county had fun
speeding like rockets down the brand new ski run.

But just near the bottom you must make a sharp turn
to avoid that backhoe as it continues to churn.
It no longer spews soil to add to the hill,
for it got stuck on an iceberg in the cold Arctic's chill.

Now it puts out ice and snow to cover the slope,
rushing thru the cavern from the other side of the globe.
But where is the neighbor, you're wondering by now?
That earth-digging auger just couldn't hold him down.

While nearing the core of the earth's central heat,
the flame from the furnace had nipped at his feet.
He retracted so fast when the fire reached his toes,
that it caused rocket fumes to rush through his nose.

He launched like spacecraft, and flew out of the hole
as Gram and Pap watched that deep-digging mole.
He slid down the hill, landing on top of the porch,
his shoe strings still burning lit the night like a torch.

Grandma and Grandpa were right thoroughly amazed;
when they tell this story people think they're just crazed.
Out on the porch that cold winter night was their aim,
to find peace and quiet from kid's with their games.

They were heard to exclaim as they piled into the den,
"That might have been fun but let's not do it again!"

The Life of Andrea
(10-4-1954 to 12-14-2009)

On an October Monday at 7:00am
she first opened her eyes to the light.
On a December Monday at 7:00pm
she closed her eyes for the night.

For the 55 years that occurred between
she was totally dedicated to God.
Most of what she did was for other people
wherever her footsteps trod.

She never married, never had a family,
though that had been one of her dreams;
she can be commemorated-on-the-mountain (Judges 11:37-
40)
with Jephthah's daughter, as the girls of Israel weep.

Andrea was a genuine Christian,
the love of her heart like fine jewels;
she selflessly gave all she had to give,
her possessions were charity's tools.

She took responsibility for her aged mother.
For her handicapped brother she fussed.
She cared for and tutored her sister's triplets.
Her business interests were left in the dust.

Her tremendous efforts brought worries and fears,
her thoughts cascading within;
it was necessary to take a break from her labors
when her delicate mind caved in.

109

She's forever free from the strain and the struggle,
but what will her family do now?
Who will be next to tend the reigns,
driving the ox and the plow?

Andrea Safron is now resting in peace,
exploring Heaven on streets of gold;
she sings with Jesus in choirs of Angels,
and basks in pleasures untold.

Wesley J. Allen
          December 16, 2009

Wildcard

Your hearing impairment isn't a handicap
as you may have once supposed;
it's a wildcard in the game of life
to enhance any hand you chose.

Many people have been dealt an ace,
specifically for their hand;
but your trump card is wild
its options are varied and grand.

If you look for ways to use it
to give your power a boost,
you'll come out shining as the chips are counted,
not whining with those who lose.

A wildcard is better than an ace,
don't be discouraged if it looks like a duce;
it has the power to make you a winner,
use it wherever you choose.

                    12-11-2009

Your Love

Your love is worth more to me than anything.
It is beautiful and precious and warm.
It is more delicious than carrot soufflé.
It is wonderful to be in your arms.

Your love shows in everything about you,
in your smile, your touch, and your beautiful face.
It makes you totally pleasing to look at.
When it's not earned, it's given by grace.

Your love feels so good it warms my heart.
It flows freely, unceasingly, leaves no doubt.
It always accepts me no matter what.
I really love you, my heart wants to shout.

It's a love that comes through the angels of God.
It is not a love set a whirl by romance.
It's a love that never leaves me or forsakes me.
It does not happen purely by chance.

I'd give all that I have to keep your love.
No price is sufficient to pay.
I give to you a love that is comparable,
a love for which one would earnestly pray.

Nothing you've given me, or that I've given you
is worth more than your precious love's touch.
I want to keep you always near me.
I love you extremely much.

6-19-2010

Turkey Day Leftovers

The stomach is full, the belly is bulging,
but still there's room for dessert.
Eat your fill, never gobble your food,
Eat slowly, talk much, and savor each word.

The gathering is great where friends share love,
an abundance of food, and a variety of dishes.
What will we do with the Turkey Day leftovers?
To see it eaten was every cook's wishes.

At special times wishes come true,
and with a group of friends like us,
we each take our share of dishes we liked,
rarely anyone puts up a fuss.

There will be cake and pie for breakfast,
turkey and salad for lunch,
veggies to keep the body functioning,
and cookies and chips for brunch.

The best part of the day was giving of thanks,
and sharing our stories with friends.
There are bits and chips of leftover trivia,
and true friendship that never ends.

11-26-2008

This poem is an answer to
George Langley's challenge
to write a poem telling what
will happen to the turkey
leftovers on Thanksgiving
Day, and use 'gobble' in
the body of the poem.

Thanks! to all my friends who
add a special delight to my life
by just being yourselves. Thanks!
for helping me to meet challenges,
conquer giants, and live above
life's pains and pitfalls. Those of
you who have poems in this book,
written about you or for you, have
told me many times that I am
a blessing to your life too.
I dedicate this book to you!

Successful
Journeys
Always,

Wesley J Allen

www.Creativeworksebooklibrary.com

www.artisticwordcreations.com

114

Made in the USA
Middletown, DE
16 June 2025

77021551R00066